THE DINOSAUR DETECTIVES IN THE SCUTTLEBUTT

BOOK TWO

STEPHANIE BAUDET

Published by Sweet Cherry Publishing Limited
Unit 36, Vulcan House
Vulcan Road
Leicester, LE5 3EF
United Kingdom

www.sweetcherrypublishing.com

First published in the UK in 2016
This edition 2017
ISBN: 978-1-78226-383-8

© Stephanie Baudet 2016

Illustrations © Allied Artists
Illustrated by Illary Casasanta
Cover design by Andrew Davis

The Dinosaur Detectives: The Scuttlebutt

Printed and bound by Wai Man Book Binding (China) Ltd, Kow-
loon, H.K.

CHAPTER ONE

'Here you are, Matt,' said Mr Sharp. 'It's very heavy.'

Matt looked at the stone item that his dad had put on the table in front of him. To anyone else it would just look like a rough lump of rock, but this was a nest of fossilised dinosaur eggs. It was impossible to separate them without damaging the eggs, so it had been agreed that they should be examined and displayed as they were.

Now it was up to Matt to identify them, using his special gift. The nest of eggs had been found in what was now southern Florida in the United States.

He sat down, closed his eyes, and rested his hands on the rounded tops of the eggs. They felt cool and rough.

Then came the shimmering, dizzy feeling that he was now used to, and soon a scene opened up in front of him. It was the sea shore, and gentle waves surged up the white sandy beach, before retreating again.

Then out of the water crawled a turtle, but one of such a size that Matt gasped in awe. It was enormous. He could see that its shell was leathery rather than solid like modern-day turtles. The twelve-foot wide creature staggered up the beach and began digging in the sand with its flippers. It was about to lay some eggs.

Matt was then aware of a brightness in the sky. He was, as yet, unable to turn and see other perspectives, but the far horizon glowed pink, and suddenly red balls of fire spewed out of one of the mountains. A volcano!

Matt was aware of something else, too. The red-hot lava had set fire to the forest, and creatures were trying to escape the flames. A great tide of dinosaurs was lumbering and running towards the sea. The sky was dark with hundreds of flying creatures that were trying to escape the choking smoke and heat.

The turtle became aware of the stampede. It turned its head, then stopped its laying, flicked a little sand over the eggs, and began trying to get back to the sea before it was trampled by the panicking dinosaurs. Matt was surprised at how fast it could move, considering how slow turtles of today were.

Even a two-tonne turtle was vulnerable against these monsters, though.

'What are they, Matt?' asked his father, as Matt slowly came back to the present.

'A huge turtle, Dad, about twelve feet across.'

'Hmm. Must be an archelon. Not really a dinosaur, but certainly from the late Cretaceous period.'

'It started to lay eggs in the sand,' said Matt, 'but a volcano was erupting and the lava had set the forest on fire. Hundreds of dinosaurs were

running to take refuge in the sea, so the archelon ran back really fast. It was amazing!'

'They were fast because their shells were not rigid, so a lot lighter,' said Dad. He lifted the egg nest off the table and staggered away with it.

'It will make a great picture, Dad,' said Matt. 'The fireballs shooting out of the volcano were spectacular, and then all the lava and flames.' Mr Sharp was not only a palaeontologist, but an artist, too, specialising in prehistoric scenes – which was called palaeo-art.

'I'm looking forward to painting it,' replied his dad, dusting his hands off after placing the egg nest somewhere safe. 'But no more work for a couple of weeks. Let's enjoy some sun and sea.'

Matt grinned and punched the air. Now that he was twelve he was allowed to go with his palaeontologist dad on egg-hunting expeditions, but this time it was a holiday and the whole family was going.

Florida. Warm sun. Sea. And some diving!

CHAPTER TWO

'When can we do some diving, Dad?' asked Matt as the whole family, Mum, Dad, sister Beth and cousin Jo, walked along the palm tree lined road in Miami. He looked at the sea longingly. It was turquoise in colour, and quite clear. So inviting.

'Why don't we go and ask about it now?' said his dad. 'There may be some reefs that we can do, and maybe a suitable diving course so you can do some wreck diving.'

'Yeah!' Matt punched the air. It was good to be on holiday with his whole family, although going with Dad on fossil-hunting expeditions was exciting, too. Well, he'd only been on one so far, to the Amazon rainforest, but now that he was twelve he would be able to go more often, as long

as they were during school holidays.

'Do you dive, Auntie Carol?' asked Jo.

Jo was Matt and Beth's cousin. Because her parents were busy doctors, she had been invited to come with them. Matt looked at her. He'd been really annoyed when she had gone to Brazil with them, but here wasn't so bad. She and his sister, Beth, got on well together, and as Beth was ten, she was only a year younger than Jo. As far as Matt knew, Jo did not scuba dive, and hopefully wasn't interested in learning.

His mum was shaking her head. 'No, Jo. I prefer swimming and maybe a bit of snorkelling.'

'Me too,' said Jo, and Matt heaved a sigh of relief. It would be just him and Dad, then.

'Why don't you three girls go and find a nice spot on the beach, or something?' said Mr Sharp. 'Matt and I will sort out some diving and we'll meet you in an hour or so?'

Matt couldn't help grinning. Things were going well.

With a wave, they split up, and Matt and his dad walked off along the quay to find the diving school. The sun was warm but not heavy and humid as it had been in Brazil.

'Looks like a marina over there, Dad.' Matt pointed.

There were a lot of boats of all shapes and sizes, some of them huge with fancy writing on the side. Miami was the home to many rich people and the place and climate were perfect for people who liked all things nautical.

A man was on one of the more modest boats, loading on scuba gear and securing scuba tanks as if preparing for a trip. The boat was called *The Esmerelda* and she was all white, and had three decks and a diving platform at the stern.

'Excuse me,' said Mr Sharp, addressing the man. 'Can you tell us where we can find out about doing some diving?'

The man was thickset and tanned, with tousled blond hair and a ready smile. He stood up straight and stretched his back, welcoming the rest from the heavy lifting. He pointed further along the quay. 'Yeah, there's Santiago's. He runs boats out to wrecks and the reef.'

'Are you preparing to go out, yourself?'

'Salvaging,' said the man. 'Probably just a scuttlebutt.' He laughed.

'A what?' said Mr Sharp.

'A scuttlebutt. A rumour. There was treasure, they said, on a wreck, but we had a look yesterday and all we found was a pile of round rocks. I'm just preparing to go out again to take another final look. Waste of time if you ask me.'

'Round rocks? How big?'

The man cupped his hands to show a four inch diameter.

Matt looked at his dad. He knew what he was thinking.

'What's the wreck?'

'She was doing the regular Miami to Nassau run. Sunk in the early thirties. I can't see what treasure she'd be carrying unless there was a rich passenger smuggling something out to the Bahamas. It was usually the other way round. It was prohibition then, and Bimini was nice and handy to get to the mainland for getting liquor. Or maybe it was payment for liquor.' He shrugged.

Mr Sharp nodded. 'Those rocks may not be the kind of treasure you were expecting, but they could well be valuable.'

The man frowned and Matt saw the funny look he gave Dad.

'I'm a palaeontologist,' said his dad. 'I study fossils. Those rocks may – just may – be dinosaur eggs.'

'You're kidding me,' said the man.

Mr Sharp shook his head. 'Can we come with you? I've had experience diving wrecks. I can probably tell you what they are before you lift them out of the water.'

The man thought for a moment. Then he nodded. 'Well, sure,' he said.

Mr Sharp took his passport out of his pocket, as well as his business card. 'I'm Alan Sharp and this is my son, Matt.'

'Welcome aboard! I'm the skipper of this ship, Steve Ashley.'

CHAPTER THREE

'You're not skippering the boat alone, are you?' asked Mr Sharp, looking round and seeing no-one.

'Hey, no!' said Steve. 'I'm just getting the gear ready to go out tomorrow.' He pointed to the sky. 'There's a squall coming this afternoon, so we delayed it, but I want to get an early start. It'll take us about four hours to get there. It's on the reef just off North Bimini. You need to be here by eight in the morning. Meantime, I'll show you round the ship.'

She was a comfortable ship, even luxurious, Matt thought. Obviously there were often rich clients who wanted only the best. The saloon area took up most of the middle deck, with the cabins below and a sundeck above. At the stern

was the lower diving platform with the air bottles lined up and secured and lockers with the rest of the scuba gear, including wetsuits.

Steve looked at Matt. 'You're not diving,' he said.

'No,' said Matt's dad before Matt could answer. 'He's got his open water certificate for ten to twelve year olds and hopes to get the next one while we're here, but obviously this is no dive for the inexperienced.'

'You'd be right there,' said Steve. 'This is a penetration dive. You experienced in that?'

Mr Sharp nodded. 'I've had a lot of experience. Not necessarily connected to my work, but as a recreational diver. I'll bring my certificates to show you, tomorrow.'

Steve nodded.

'Just one thing,' said Mr Sharp. 'How come no-one has dived the wreck before?'

'Oh, did I forget to say? It's prohibited. It's right on the edge of the abyss that drops to around 6 thousand feet.'

'Ah,' said Mr Sharp.

Matt felt a sudden shiver of fear. 6000 feet was scary, although the deepest part of the ocean was a staggering 36000. Just the thought of all that water was terrifying. What if the wreck moved when Dad and the divers were inside? What if it toppled over the edge, taking them with it?

He looked up at Dad, who was smiling as he shook hands with Steve, and they clambered off the boat.

They found Santiago's Diving School further along the quay and booked some more advanced

lessons for Matt, including some shallow wreck diving. There were several old ships that had been purposely sunk for recreational diving and for gaining experience.

Despite his fears, Matt couldn't wait until the

next day. Even though he wouldn't be able to dive the wreck, if there were dinosaur eggs down there; it would be an unexpected addition to their holiday.

One thing threatened to spoil the trip, and again, like the expedition to Brazil, it was called Jo.

They met up with the girls and Matt excitedly told them about Steve and the search for 'treasure'.

'Those dinosaur eggs follow you round,' said Mrs Sharp, shaking her head. 'Or else you can sniff them out. Can't we just have a holiday and leave the dinosaurs behind? These fossils have been where they are for millions of years, and all of a sudden you have to go digging them out now.'

'Oh, but Mum,' said Matt. 'These haven't been there that long, and this guy was ready to give up. He thought they were just rocks.'

'They may well be,' said his dad. 'It's only one day, love,' he said to his wife.

'If they are dinosaur eggs, who will they belong to?' asked Jo.

'Well, I'm not sure,' said Mr Sharp. 'I think salvagers have a right to some of the proceeds, but that's up to the US authorities. I'll make sure they are reported to the right people.'

As Steve had predicted, there was a tropical

storm later that afternoon. No thunder and lightning, but torrential rain that thundered down for several hours, so that roads and pavements became temporary rivers.

There was nothing to do but go back to the hotel and watch some TV. They found some old board games in the lounge. He was surprised that he actually enjoyed them, although they couldn't have been more different from the games he usually played on his tablet.

Thankfully, the next morning was calm and clear. Mum and Beth were going shopping, but not Jo. All girls liked shopping, didn't they? But oh no – Jo wanted to come along on the boat.

'It'll be exciting for the divers, but we'll just be waiting on board,' said Matt, but he couldn't put her off.

'I'll just go for the ride,' she said. 'I've never been out on the ocean on a boat before.'

Steve seemed a little anxious at seeing two children climbing aboard. He frowned.

'Oh, they're good kids,' said Mr Sharp, winking quickly at Matt and Jo. 'In fact, they both came with me on my last fossil-hunting expedition to Brazil.'

'You're kidding me,' said Steve. 'In all that jungle? Rather you than me.'

There were two other men on board. One was a diver, introduced as Mac, and the other man, Jim, would help with their equipment and then stay on the ship while the divers explored the wreck. They looked at Mr Sharp and the children with raised eyebrows.

'I don't think they're convinced about your dinosaur egg theory.' Steve laughed. 'And neither were any of the guys I told in the bar last night. If you're wrong, I'll never live it down.'

'It'll make a good story, either way, your scuttlebutt,' said Dad.

'It sure will.' Steve didn't look like the kind of guy who would be bothered by some teasing by

his mates. 'But I brought on board some lifting gear. Those rocks are heavy.'

Matt had seen the winch on the side of the diving platform at the stern. He glanced at it now, and noticed that the boat next to them was leaving, too. She was much smaller, but the two men on board, while getting the boat ready for departure, seemed to be watching them rather closely. He thought about Dad's jealous colleague, Frank Hellman, who seemed intent on getting his hands on the fossilised dinosaur eggs and selling them on for profit.

But he couldn't be here, could he? They were on holiday. There was no reason that Frank would have been watching Dad here in Florida. Anyway, neither of those men were Frank. Matt would certainly recognise him again!

In the meantime, if these were dinosaur eggs, what kind of dinosaur could they be? The continents had changed a lot since the time of the dinosaurs. Originally there was just one super continent, called Pangaea, but around 200 million years ago, in the Triassic era, it had begun to split apart, eventually forming the continents we know today. Matt knew that where they were standing right now may well have been under water, and where the wreck was located may have been land. So the dinosaur who laid the eggs could have been a true dinosaur, or a prehistoric aquatic creature, depending on where the owner of the eggs found them.

Whatever it was, what were they doing on a ship? Payment for the liquor, maybe, as Steve had suggested. Matt had taken a chance during the storm to do a bit of research on what Steve had mentioned the day before. Prohibition, they had called it. It was a complete ban on alcohol in the US during the 1920s and 1930s. Those who could get their hands on some would make a lot of money by selling it on, and Matt had already learnt from Frank that people would do anything to fill their pockets.

CHAPTER FOUR

'The wreck is just off the coast of one of the Bimini Islands,' explained Steve as they got underway. 'It's in about sixty feet of water. Now, before we get too far, regulations say we have to go through lifeboat drill.'

'There's not going to be another storm, is there?' asked Jo.

'Not according to the weather forecast,' said Steve, 'but unexpected things can happen. Fire, for one. Now, we have two thirty-foot tenders, each with outboard engines. They are often used when we can't get the ship close enough to the reefs, or to shore, but they are our lifeboats, too.'

Matt frowned for a moment and looked at Jo. She seemed just as confused as him. Mr Sharp, on seeing their faces, swiftly pointed at the two small boats on the side of the ship – big enough to hold their crew and maybe a few more.

'I want you to listen up,' he continued. 'We'll be passing over a place where a ship went down in 1965 and ninety people died. One of them was my uncle. The high death toll was because they had no fire drill.'

Matt saw the sadness in his eyes, even after all these years. 'What happened?'

'There was a fire,' said Steve. 'It was in the middle of the night because this ship was doing a regular run from Miami to Nassau. She was an old ship, originally called *The Esmerelda*, like this one, but they changed the name to the *Yarmouth Castle*, and that's considered unlucky.

'Because she was old, she'd been painted many times and the paint on the lifeboat ropes was so thick, they wouldn't slide through the winches, so most of the boats couldn't be lowered.'

'That's awful!' Jo said.

'Not only that, but the crew were lax and had no safety training, so it was chaos. The captain and some of his officers were the first ones off the ship in one of the few lifeboats they were able to launch.'

'I can hardly believe that could happen,' said Matt's dad. 'So relatively recently.'

'The one good thing that came out of it,' went on Steve, 'was that the Safety of Life at Sea law was passed in 1966, requiring fire drills and safety inspections on all ships worldwide, no matter where they are registered.'

He went on to show them where to meet in the event of a fire, where the fire extinguishers were kept and how to operate them.

Matt couldn't believe that, even though they would be surrounded by so much water, fire could be a real danger. You had to be brave to be the captain on a ship!

'Okay, so this is the drill. Use the acronym F.I.R.E.' He counted on his fingers.

'**F** ind the fire, location and size.

I nform the captain.

R estrict the fire.

E xtinguish the fire.'

Then he went into detail about each one of the points.

Later, Matt asked Steve. 'Has anyone been down to the wreck of that ship?'

'*Yarmouth Castle*?' Steve shook his head. 'She's far too deep for divers to go, at 1800 feet, and I think we should leave the dead to rest in peace.'

'Did anyone die on the wreck we're going to now?'

'No. Like the *Yarmouth Castle*, it was a regular passenger ship between the US and the Bahamas, but it hit the reef in a storm, and everyone was rescued.'

They arrived at the site, marked by a red and white buoy, just after twelve o'clock.

'What a wonderful place,' said Mr Sharp. 'Ideal for diving. Maybe we ought to come here for a couple of days, Matt. Your mum would love it.'

They all looked at the clear, turquoise sea sloshing beneath them, and the low-lying island just visible on the horizon, with its strip of white sand.

'You're right, buddy, it sure is a great place,' said Steve. 'As well as the reef there are plenty of wrecks to dive, some of them sunk on purpose.'

Dad nodded and grinned at Matt.

Steve hoisted up the red and white dive flag. 'Shows other boats that we have divers likely to surface,' he said. 'Right, let's get going.'

Matt and Jo watched as Dad, Steve and the other diver, Mac, got into their wetsuits and fins and hoisted the air tanks onto their backs. Then, after fitting their mouthpieces and masks, they went carefully through the pre-dive check, examining each other's equipment thoroughly before jumping into the ocean.

'How long will they be?' asked Jo, watching the air bubbles bursting on the surface.

Matt looked at her. He couldn't imagine why she had come – she had sat with her hand clutching the deck rail for the entire journey out. He tried not to show his annoyance.

'They can only stay down about half an hour,' he said. 'Then they have to make some short stops coming up so they don't get decompression sickness.'

She accepted that. No questions. And anyway, Matt was not going to give her a lesson in dive tables and decompression hazards.

'I'm going to get a drink,' he said.

'Bring me one, too,' said Jo, sitting back in a deck chair.

Matt gritted his teeth and carried on towards the kitchen.

Since the divers had no cameras, there was nothing for Matt and Jo to do but wait, and enjoy the sunshine.

Matt had just got back with the drinks when his phone buzzed. It was Mum.

'Hi Mum. Yes, they've just gone down. It's really nice here. We're right near North Bimini Island. Dad says we should all come here for a couple of days. You could snorkel. The reefs are amazing.'

When he'd finished the call, Jo said, 'How do you know the reefs are amazing? You haven't seen them.'

'I looked up Bimini on my phone.'

Jo looked at him and their eyes met. She giggled and Matt couldn't help but smile, despite himself.

Then, from behind them, they heard the winch winding up.

'Dad must think they're dinosaur eggs,' exclaimed Matt. He leapt from the chair and dashed to the stern of the boat to where Jim was operating the winch. The 'treasure' would reach the surface before the divers, who would have to make a few short decompression stops on the way up. Or maybe there were more eggs and they were sending them in more than one lot.

All three waited for the basket to break the surface.

When it did, Matt gasped. 'Yes!' he said, looking at the familiar shapes.

Jim hauled the basket in, carefully lifted out the stones, and then lowered it back into the water again.

'Do you think there are more?' asked Matt.

'I reckon,' said Jim. He poked at the stones. 'Don't look like no eggs to me.'

'They're fossilised,' said Matt.

'Right.' He frowned.

It was then that Matt sensed a presence behind him, and turned.

Two men stood there, and Matt staggered back in surprise, knowing something was wrong. He didn't know much about protocol at sea but he did know that you asked permission to step aboard someone's ship.

Jim jumped and frowned. 'You're trespassin',' he growled.

'And we'll have those, thank you,' said one, pointing at the eggs.

It was the two men from the boat that had been moored next to them back at the quay in Miami. They were in wetsuits, and had obviously swam from wherever their boat was and sneaked aboard stealthily while they had all been looking at the contents of the basket.

They both had one hand on what looked like a waterproof holster attached to their belts. Matt

suspected they had guns, but in any case, no-one was going to argue with two guys built like heavyweight prize fighters. Definitely not one boat-hand and two children!

'Cell phones,' said the second man, holding out his hand.

Jo and Jim handed theirs over. Matt shook his head. 'I left mine with my sister, in Miami,' he lied.

'Search the lockers,' said the first man. 'The other guys must have phones with their stuff, too.'

Matt stole a quick glance at Jo, who smiled reassuringly, and he silently thanked her for not having given him away on the phone thing.

While he watched, scowling, the second man quickly found another three phones and then flung them all overboard. He strode over to Matt, and since Matt was only wearing shorts and a t-shirt the body search didn't take long.

Then the man stepped back and stared at Matt, as if unable to believe someone didn't have a phone. Matt stared right back but his heart thumped wildly.

'Okay, you three, get into the saloon,' said the first man. 'And we'll wait here until the next load of treasure comes up.'

Matt thought of scoffing at the word 'treasure' but these men weren't stupid. They knew what the treasure was, and somehow they *had* to be connected to Frank Hellman. Although it seemed amazing that Hellman had known where they were, and that they were aboard this boat salvaging the dinosaur eggs, it would be even more of a coincidence if it were someone else. Matt did remember, though, that Steve had said he mentioned the possibility of the stones being dinosaur eggs in the bar last night. That was a silly thing to do, Matt thought, although most people wouldn't know a dinosaur egg if they were hit by one.

He made a mental note to ask Dad if this kind

of thing had happened to him before. Was there always so much rivalry between palaeontologists?

The three of them sat in the saloon, feeling helpless. Matt wondered what would happen when Dad and the others surfaced. These men would be outnumbered then, but they did have the advantage of surprise, as well as the fact that the divers would still have all their diving gear attached. There was also the fact that they were probably armed.

Jo looked at him as if reading the thoughts that were buzzing through his mind. She didn't look surprised when Matt said, 'I'm going down to warn them.'

Matt had learnt that Jo was not one to try to dissuade someone who had made a decision, and she was willing to help in any way she could. It was Jim who jumped to his feet, shaking his head.

'No! No way, kid. I didn't ask to be no babysitter, but I do as Steve says if I want to keep my job.'

'I can dive,' said Matt. 'I have my open water certificate and I'm not going to penetrate the wreck.'

'You've dived to sixty feet before?'

'Well, no, but look, we can't just let these guys steal the eggs, they're worth a fortune.'

'And someone could get really hurt if Matt doesn't warn them!' Jo added.

'Eggs! Stones!' said Jim. 'They don't look like much to me.'

'Treasure isn't always sparkly!' Matt said, losing patience, but then wondering if he'd gone too far.

'What are these men going to do when they've got the eggs? They'll probably smash up the boat at the very least.'

Jim looked hard at him. 'You're a brave kid. I'd go if I could, but I can't dive any more. Problem with my ears.' He touched his ears to make his point.

'Help me, then.'

'The thing is,' said Jim. 'The tanks are on the diving deck, right where those guys are.'

Matt's heart sank. Of course they were! How could they possibly sneak out there and grab all the gear, including a heavy air tank?

CHAPTER FIVE

Time was running out. The divers would be surfacing soon. If only Matt could warn them! There was a chance of the eggs being saved as well as the villains being overpowered – but Matt was sure they had guns. He hadn't seen them yet, but these guys didn't seem the type to ask nicely.

Then Jim spoke. 'I have an idea, Matt. If I cause some sort of diversion, could you climb over from the upper deck onto the diving platform and get the gear? You'd have to be quick.'

'I'll try,' said Matt, nodding.

'I'll pretend to have a fight with Jo,' he said. 'I won't hurt you,' he added, looking at Jo, who seemed a bit worried. 'We have to make it look real, though. Maybe I'll start the engine and you try to stop me.'

Matt crept quietly up the steps to the deck above. Suddenly, he heard the engine start up, accompanied by shouting, and Jo screamed so convincingly that he almost turned back.

But he only hesitated for a moment. Then he was at the stern of the boat just above the diving platform.

Cautiously, he leaned over.

There was only one man in sight. He was looking back towards the bridge where there were still raised voices and the sound of the engine.

Then it appeared that the line attached to the winch moved because he peered over the side intently.

Matt climbed over the rail, reaching for a foothold somewhere. This had to be done quickly and quietly.

He had taken off his shoes, and now his toes felt a small ledge on the side of the boat. One slip and he would not only fail, but he'd fall into the sea. Not that he couldn't swim, but what if they punished him by not letting him back aboard?

Then the engine cut and there was silence again, but he was down and creeping towards the air tanks. For a moment the second man looked back towards the interior of the boat, where there were still raised voices. Matt ducked behind the tanks. From there he could release one.

Now, he needed fins and mask from the lockers – best to get those first before releasing the air tank, which was going to be heavy.

There was some particularly loud shouting coming from the saloon and the man on the diving platform went to the door and looked in.

Matt opened a locker and grabbed a pair of fins and mask, hung them over one arm, and managed to close the locker again so as not to give himself away. Then he quietly released an air tank and slung it loosely onto his back. How was he ever going to lift all this up? It was impossible. Any minute the second man would turn, or the first man would be back and would see him. Then it would all be over.

Then he had a better idea. Instead of climbing back up to the deck above, hauling the heavy tank, what if he could walk along the edge of the rail and get past the supporting strut? That way he could stay on the same deck but further round, behind the saloon.

Thankful that the sea was calm, and that the varnished wooden rail wasn't wet, Matt climbed onto it. Then he stepped sideways, gripping onto anything he could with his one free arm. He heard the first man coming back, cursing and grumbling.

'I thought I felt a tug on the line,' said the second man.

'Three tugs is the signal, not one,' said the other. 'Probably some big fish bumped it. Maybe even a shark.' He chuckled.

Matt swallowed. Of course there were sharks here.

Then Jo appeared, looking rather pale, and reached out to help him. 'He tied Jim up,' she said. 'Tied him to the chair.'

'Is he okay?' Matt asked and Jo nodded. 'Help me get this gear on. I couldn't get a wetsuit and they'd be too big, anyway.'

Soon he had on the fins, and the tank secured to his back. Just the mouthpiece and mask now.

He should go through the pre-dive check, which was usually done with a buddy, but, since Jo knew nothing about scuba diving, he would have to do it alone. Jim had dived in the past, but Matt couldn't afford the time to go into the saloon and risk being seen.

'Hurry!' urged Jo.

'I have to check the equipment,' said Matt. 'Look, I can't use the dive platform so going over the rail is going to make a big splash …'

'I thought of that,' she said, 'I'll go into the galley and drop something just as you hit the water.'

Buoyancy compensator, check the release, the tank – valve open. Matt tried hard to remember the checklist, but at the same time aware of the time slipping by.

Finally, he put on his mask and mouthpiece. Then he clambered up onto the boat rail and waited until Jo was in the galley.

She gave him a wave, saucepan in hand.

Matt toppled backwards into the warm sea.

CHAPTER SIX

Without weights it was going to take him about thirty seconds to get down to the wreck – and that was the deepest he had ever dived. The open water certificate he had was only to forty feet and Matt was hoping to go the next stage during this holiday. That would take him to sixty feet.

That was with an instructor and with other people around. One of the most important rules in diving was never to do it alone. Always have a diving buddy so you could watch out for each other.

He knew this had been a crazy idea, and Dad would probably be quite angry, but Matt was determined to thwart Frank Hellman and his mates. Also, he had no way of knowing just how ruthless they were. There was the chance that

Dad, Steve or any of them, could get seriously hurt. These men were not playing games.

All he could hear was his own breathing as he took in each breath and then the air bubbled out. A shoal of small fish swarmed towards him, trying to scare him off. He could feel their small teeth nibbling at his t-shirt. As long as it was only small fish. There were sharks here, lots of them, and also stingrays. He didn't really think that either of these things would try to attack him if he didn't provoke them, but that was easy to say when you were up on dry land. Being alone down here was both beautiful and terrifying.

Being noon, the sun was directly overhead, and its rays were making it easy for Matt to see. If he looked up he could still see the hull of the boat, and, looking towards the ocean floor, he could just make out the dark angular shape of the wreck against the reef.

That was on one side. On the other side all he could see was dark blue. The abyss, where the ocean floor dropped away to four thousand feet.

The wreck was literally teetering on the edge and any small undersea quake could send it toppling over to disappear forever, along with anyone inside.

Matt could feel his heart thudding. Maybe he should just go back now, but he knew that it would take him longer to ascend than it did to descend. This was no place to panic. Divers had to be calm and sensible, and ascending required several short stops to decompress and dispel the nitrogen from their blood.

He reached the wreck and stood on the deck, looking round. There was no sign of any divers. Matt could see that the basket attached to the winch line was lying empty.

The wreck tilted to one side. Much of the superstructure had rusted away leaving the upper decks open, but this was a sizeable ship,

with several decks. Metal steps led down through what had once been a door.

The opening was narrow, with only just enough room for a person and their air tank. Matt suddenly felt really afraid at the thought of entering such a small environment. Penetration dives were not for the beginner. They were dangerous. One reason was that you could get snagged on something, and another was that you could get lost and not be able to find your way out. Divers usually had guide ropes, but he couldn't see any here. Maybe they had found another entrance.

Meanwhile, what was going on in the boat above? Had the men discovered that he was missing?

Matt had an idea – two, in fact.

The first was that he would bang on the hull of the wreck. That should bring Dad and the others out without him having to go in.

He found a flat area on the metal hull and hit it with his hand. It hardly made any sound at all. He would have to find something hard to use.

He swam away from the wreck and down onto the reef. The coral was sharp so he had to be careful not to brush against it as he swam along, looking for a suitable thing to use. He would never break off a piece of the precious coral. He stopped and grabbed what seemed to be half of a dead shellfish shell, picking up a handful of seaweed and sand in the process.

Back on the deck again, he banged three times on a metal strut and heard the deep tones reverberating inside. Then he banged three more times.

For a moment he wondered whether anyone had heard – but surely they must have? Then a diver appeared some distance away but he couldn't tell who it was. He waved. The diver swam towards him, followed by the other two.

It was Dad, and although Matt couldn't see his expression through the mask, he could tell by his body language that he was confused and angry. Matt pointed upwards, trying to remember the sign language for danger above. Why hadn't he thought of it before? How stupid. He could have been thinking about it on the way down.

He knew the sign for aborting the dive – a hand across the throat … then he had it! A clenched fist meant danger. He clenched his fist and pointed his arm up towards the surface.

With relief, Dad immediately understood and nodded. If Steve and Mac wondered what it was all about, they had no way of asking, and fortunately did not try to argue with the decision

to end the dive – and Steve was in charge, after all.

Matt's second idea was to give three tugs on the winch line, but not before they had completed their decompression stops and were almost at the surface. Watching for what was coming up in the basket would occupy the men's attention while he, Dad and the other two climbed aboard.

As they took their first stop, though, Matt noticed something. Above their heads was a shape, a very familiar grey shape and it seemed to be circling. Then Matt looked down, his arm was bleeding.

CHAPTER SEVEN

Matt had no idea what to do, apart from not panic. Steve swam over, grasped Matt's t-shirt with both hands, and tore it off. Then he bound it around the wound on his arm to stem the bleeding.

Mac motioned them all to stay still and not to wave their limbs about. Matt had watched a TV show about sharks with Beth once. The advice had been to be still, but not to play dead either.

They all watched the shark as it zig-zagged in front of them.

Steve pointed to his watch, indicating that it was time to ascend further. There was nowhere to hide from the shark.

Matt couldn't see any blood coming from his arm, now, but he knew that sharks could smell even the smallest amount from miles away, let alone a few yards in front.

At the next stop the shark came very close. Matt could clearly see the rows of sharp teeth in its hideous mouth. He felt light-headed and could hear his breathing become erratic. Mac gripped him and looked into his face through the mask. His own face showed a stoic calmness, which helped Matt. He was on the verge of all-out panic. He knew that common sense and his small amount of diving training were losing the battle, and there would come a point when he would just lose it altogether. Mac used his fingers to tell Matt to direct his eyes at him. Then he calmly used his hand to indicate slower breathing, *in-out, in-out.*

Matt took a deep breath. He could hear a strange moaning sound that he realised was coming from him.

The shark came closer.

Matt wanted to close his eyes, but he couldn't.

Then, out of nowhere, and making Matt jolt with shock, Steve lunged forward and a wash of bubbles and water surrounded them. He struck the shark on the nose and then in the eye with something he had in his hand.

The shark quivered and backed off a little way.

When it came round again, Steve was waiting. The shark hung there for a few seconds, then it changed its mind and swam away, leaving a wispy trail of its own blood, mingling with Matt's.

The four of them visibly relaxed and gave the thumbs up sign. But then Matt pointed upwards again and cautioned, finger to mouth, for stealth. Of course, Steve and Mac wouldn't have any idea what the problem could be, but thank goodness they seemed to trust Matt. Maybe Dad would have some idea, although who would have imagined that Frank Hellman would have followed them

here? If it *was* Frank Hellman. Since Dad had been awarded his MBE, there were a lot of people and professors who knew his name.

They could see the surface now, and the hull of the boat, with the winch line stretching down to the bottom. Now was the time to give them the signal. Matt grabbed the rope and tugged three times. Then, as it began to move, he motioned to the others to surface nearer the front of the boat rather than the diving platform at the stern. It would be impossible to board the boat from anywhere else, but they would be able to take the men by surprise. Unfortunately, Jim was out of action, being tied up.

They surfaced, and there was Jo, hanging over the side. She flung over a rope ladder, and once more Matt mentally applauded her as she helped to haul him into the boat, where he hurriedly took out his mouthpiece.

'Dad,' Matt panted. 'I think it's Frank Hellman's men. They're stealing the eggs and they have tied Jim to a chair. They might be armed, too.'

'They *will* be armed,' said Steve, 'whoever they are. How many of them, Matt?'

'Two.'

As quietly as they could, the four of them clambered up the rope ladder, but before they could haul it in another diver appeared from over the side, and another. Then more men were coming from the stern of the boat.

It seemed that there were more than two men, after all.

The air tanks were snatched off their backs.

'You can leave your fins on,' said one man. 'You can't run far in those, even if you can undo the ropes we tie you up with.' He turned towards the rear of the boat and shouted. 'Those other eggs come up yet, Chas?'

'You're not going to like this, boss.' One of the

original men appeared. 'It's empty.'

The boss glared at Matt's dad, who had a slight gleam of triumph in his eye.

'You Sharp?' asked the boss.

'Yes.'

'Any more of these rocks down there?'

'You'll have to go and see for yourself,' said Mr Sharp. 'Did Frank send you?'

The boss ignored the question but glowered at them all. His gaze stopped at Matt.

'One thing I'll say for you, sonny. You're a brave kid, although it got you absolutely nowhere.'

Matt wasn't sure whether praise from a villain counted for much, but this man was right about the failure bit. His dive had been for nothing.

In a matter of minutes, a small boat had moored alongside and all the men had gone, taking the first lot of dinosaur eggs with them. They tied all six of them up before they left, but they helped each other, and as soon Steve was free he ran for the bridge. But he was soon back.

'They've smashed the radio. Anyone got a cell phone?'

'They took our phones,' said Matt, 'except that I hid mine in one of the tenders.' He ran to get it.

'No signal,' he said, returning.

'Look,' said Steve, 'we could put into port here

in Bimini, but there's nothing wrong with the boat. I'm making the decision to head back to Miami. We should get a cell phone signal before long and we can alert the authorities. Those guys won't get far.'

They weighed anchor and started the engine. Matt took off his wet clothes and spread them out on the deck to dry. Steve had given him a bathrobe to wear in the meantime.

Much later, when they were about halfway back to Miami, there *was* a phone signal and Steve sent a message to the police and coast guard, although he wasn't sure whether it got through or not.

'There isn't much to go on,' he said. 'We don't know what their boat is like as we were tied up inside the cabin. I mentioned dinosaur eggs, but I have a feeling they'll think I'm some kinda nut. You sure they *are* dinosaur eggs, Alan?'

'I can't be sure,' said Mr Sharp, 'but why else would there be round rocks in someone's cabin on a ship?'

'You got a point,' said Steve.

Just then, two things happened. One was that dark clouds began to rumble up and the wind gusted threateningly.

'Looks like we're in for a storm,' said Mac. 'They can suddenly come outta nowhere in this part of the world.'

The second thing was that the engine suddenly spluttered and died.

CHAPTER EIGHT

'Sea anchor!' yelled Steve. 'Let's get her into the wind if we can.'

Meanwhile, Mac went to take a look at the engine.

'I feel so helpless,' said Mr Sharp to Matt and Jo. 'I do know that without an engine we're at the mercy of the waves. Let's hope Mac gets it going again.'

Matt noticed the worried frown on his face.

'That's what the sea anchor is for, Alan,' said Steve, overhearing. 'It causes a drag and stabilises the boat to some extent. If we can get her round facing into the wind it should keep us stable.'

Mac came back, shaking his head. 'No gas,' he said. 'Tanks are empty.'

Steve gritted his teeth. 'I thought they let us off

lightly,' he said. 'Leave us just enough to get well away from land and then leave us drifting. Gives them more time to get away.'

The wind was really blowing now, squalling, buffeting the boat as though it was a piece of driftwood.

'Everyone below!' shouted Steve. 'Let's batten down everything and ride it out. Alan, can you try to get through to the coastguard on Matt's cell phone? No-one's gonna come out in this, though.'

Matt felt a little queasy as the boat rocked about. But there was something else, too. He was sure he could smell smoke. Or was it his imagination?

He scrambled down the stairway, grabbing hold of the handrails tightly as the boat pitched.

F.I.R.E.

F.   Find the location of it.

In such a small boat that wasn't difficult. Smoke curled from under the door of one of the forward cabins.

I.   Inform the captain.

'Steve!' he shouted, scrambling back up the stairway as fast as he could.

If they followed the drill as it was written, they

61

should have assembled on deck, but because of the weather they crowded into the saloon.

'You three stay here, please,' said Steve, addressing Matt, Jo and Mr Sharp. 'We can deal with this. There's not too much room down there.'

He, Mac and Jim grabbed extinguishers and ran, in fact, slid down the stairway.

'How come the fire just started now?' asked Jo.

'Those guys delayed it somehow,' said Mr Sharp. 'Don't worry, Jo. Steve and the guys will put it out.'

The boat was really pitching now, her bows rising into the waves, which crashed and splattered over the forward deck. Matt was getting very worried, although he tried not to show it. He wondered what Mum and Beth were doing. Was it stormy in Miami, or just here, at sea?

He tried to remember the last things Mum had said, and the last thing he had said to her. He tried to gauge the danger from Dad's face but wasn't sure whether he was trying to look calm for their sake.

'There's smoke drifting up the stairway,' said Jo, quietly, and Matt and his dad looked. It was true. Were they losing the battle? How much damage could a fire do on board a steel ship?

That *Yarmouth Castle* had had a steel hull, but everything on the inside and the deck itself were wooden, so far more flammable.

At least there are two tenders, thought Matt, although he didn't fancy abandoning ship in this storm. Surely the boat could never *sink*? He clung onto a metal strut to stop himself from being flung off the seat. The nausea was getting worse, but he was afraid to move.

He saw his dad looking at him and then getting up and struggling towards the galley, soon coming back with a big plastic bowl. With a small smile, he thrust it at Matt and then slumped back onto the chair. Jo sat close to her uncle, paler even than before, but she smiled a small smile at Matt. The seconds seemed to pass by slowly as they waited for the rest of the crew, afraid that they might not return at all.

Steve appeared at the stairway, coughing and gasping for breath. 'Help us with Mac. Fumes …'

Mr Sharp sprang up and followed him down the stairs.

Jo looked at Matt.

Now there were four of them down there in the danger zone.

Then it was Mr Sharp and Jim who dragged Mac up the stairs, tottering from side to side as

the boat pitched. They laid him on the floor of the saloon. Mac was a funny colour and Matt couldn't even tell if he was breathing. Mr Sharp felt in Mac's neck for a pulse, then bent to give him some mouth-to-mouth resuscitation.

Mac convulsed and then took in a deep breath. His eyes opened and he looked around, confused.

Steve knelt at his side. 'You're okay, Mac. It was the fumes of the fire. You're gonna be okay. We got the fire out, anyway.'

'What caused the fire?' asked Jo.

'Those guys …' began Steve. Then he looked up at Mr Sharp. 'Who *are* those guys, Alan?'

Mr Sharp's brows furrowed and his mouth was hard set. Matt could tell the look of exasperation on his face. 'I'm sorry to have caused this,' Mr Sharp said. 'It's a rival palaeontologist, I'm sure. He wants to get the dinosaur eggs for the money and the credit, without doing the work – and he wants to get back at me. Past jealousies. It's a long story.'

'He sure means business,' said Jim.

'But …' said Jo, looking puzzled. 'Why didn't we notice the fire before? Did they delay it?'

Jim smiled, grimly. 'A bit of fuse wire will do it. They were banking on no-one going into that cabin and discovering their contraptions.'

The storm was easing. Matt took a deep breath and hoped he wasn't going to throw up. He hated throwing up, and it would be embarrassing, too. He took his phone out of his pocket. It was nearly six o'clock. Mum and Beth would be expecting them back any minute. The phone buzzed, making him almost drop it in surprise.

'It's Mum! There's a signal.'

It was a text.

'Don't worry her,' said his dad. 'Just say we've been held up by some engine trouble, but we hope to be rescued soon. Tell her to check that the coastguard got our message.'

'We need to contact them so that they can get our GPS position,' said Jim, reaching for Matt's phone as soon as he'd sent the text. 'Even if they got our last one we might have drifted a bit during the storm, despite the sea anchor.'

'Can we send up a flare?' asked Matt.

Steve shook his head. 'They're for emergencies only. We're quite safe. They'll find us as soon as the weather clears.'

They did. Within an hour a coastguard boat drew up alongside and Steve explained that all they needed was fuel.

'The cops have got an APB out on those guys,' said the coastguard.

'Oh, our message got through, then?'

'Yup.' He looked round. 'What did they take? It sounded like fossils.'

Mr Sharp nodded. 'We think they're dinosaur eggs.'

The coastguard's eyes grew large. 'You don't say!' he said.

Matt laughed. 'My dad's a palaeontologist,' he said, proudly.

'You don't say!' said the coastguard again.

Chapter Nine

Matt cupped his hands around the stone, feeling its shape and weight beneath his sensitive fingers. Then the dizziness began.

'It might be a plesiosaur's egg,' he heard his father say, as if from a distance.

Matt shook his head. 'Aren't they live breeders?'

He didn't hear what his father replied because he was there, on a sandy shore. The sea was calm and clear with hardly a ripple. Such a peaceful scene. But when he looked towards the land, it was a scene of devastation. The vegetation was blackened right to the shore. The fire he'd seen in his last vision had ripped through, burning everything in its path, including the animals that could not escape.

But it was not a turtle's egg that he was holding

this time. The creature that basked in the shallow water was a mosasaur, with its long, pointed head and very powerful jaws, which it now opened to snap on a fish. The teeth were sharp and there were lots of them.

Not exactly a dinosaur, but a prehistoric marine sea lizard – a marine reptile, his dad would have said – that breathed air and crawled up onto the beach to lay its eggs.

It was a giant of an animal, and Matt stepped back – something he had not been able to do before – as it swam powerfully to the shore and emerged, all thirty feet of it. Matt was glad that it couldn't see him. Whether or not it would have considered him a good meal, he didn't know, but he was sure it might have tried anyway. They were carnivores.

It hardly seemed possible that the egg he held in his hand could produce such an enormous creature.

Matt slowly came back to the present. His dad was still standing in front of him, his eyebrows raised questioningly.

'It's a mosasaur.'

His dad nodded. 'Probably *Mosasaur plotosaurus*. Fossils have been found in North America. Not as big as the European variety at sixty feet long.'

Matt grinned. 'You really wouldn't want to meet one of these, either, Dad.'

The eggs were handed over to the American Natural History Museum, but Steve did receive a salvage fee, too. Matt was glad. After all, his boat had been damaged and they'd all had a scary experience.

The egg thieves had been apprehended in Nassau, in the Bahamas, trying to board a flight to Europe. Sure enough, they admitted to being employees of Frank Hellman, who appeared to have spies everywhere. It seemed that man had more money than sense, and would do anything to get back at Mr Sharp for his fame and achievements.

One of the policemen who had apprehended them and brought back the eggs, spoke to Matt's dad. 'He had a message for you, sir.'

'I think I know what that message is,' said Mr Sharp. 'He's not giving up.'

'That's about it,' said the policeman.

'Is there always this kind of rivalry between palaeontologists, Dad?' asked Matt.

'Maybe normal professional rivalry,' said Mr Sharp, 'but not usually so ruthless, although there was a famous case in America in the nineteenth century, known as *The Bone Wars*.

Both paleontologists used their wealth and influence to finance their own expeditions and soon they were financially and socially ruined by their attempts to disgrace each other, but their contributions to the field of paleontology were massive. *The Bone Wars* gave us a lot of knowledge of prehistoric life.'

'Now I don't want any more talk of dinosaurs, or fossils or eggs,' said Matt's mum. 'This is a holiday!'

It was the morning after their adventure, and they were sitting down to breakfast.

Just then the waitress came over to their table and smiled. 'Hi there! How would you folks like your eggs this morning? Over easy, or sunny side up?'

She wondered why they all burst out laughing.